TRIPP SCHOOL
850 HIGHLAND GROVE
BUFFALO GROVE, IL 60089

SAGUARO CACTUS

PAUL AND SHIRLEY BERQUIST

℘ **Children's Press**

A Division of Grolier Publishing
New York London Hong Kong Sydney
Danbury, Connecticut

Created and Developed by The Learning Source

Designed by Josh Simons

Acknowledgment: We would like to thank Saguaro National Park and the other organizations that provided technical assistance with this project. Their help is greatly appreciated.

All illustrations by Glenn Quist

Photo Credits: Gerry Ellis/Ellis Nature Photography: 29; All other photos: Paul and Shirley Berquist.

Printed in the United States of America.
1 2 3 4 5 6 7 8 9 10 R 06 05 04 03 02 01 00 99 98 97

Library of Congress Cataloging-in-Publication Data
Berquist, Paul and Shirley.
　　Saguaro cactus / by Paul and Shirley Berquist.
　　　　p.　　cm. — (Habitats)
　　Summary: Describes the size, life, and potential age span of the saguaro cactus and its effect on other desert life.
　　　ISBN 0-516-20713-X　　　(0-516-26065-0 pbk.)
　　　1. Saguaro—Juvenile literature. 2. Saguaro—Ecology—Sonoran Desert Juvenile Literature. 3. Desert ecology—Sonoran Desert—Juvenile literature.
[1. Saguaro. 2. Cactus. 3. Desert ecology. 4. Ecology.] I. Title. II. Series: Habitats (Childrens Press)
OK495.C11B42 1997
583'.56—dc21,　　　　　　　　　　　　　96-37097
　　　　　　　　　　　　　　　　　　　　　　　　CIP
　　　　　　　　　　　　　　　　　　　　　　　　AC

The Sonoran Desert is a small bit of land in the southwestern United States. The weather is hot and dry there for most of the year. It is a very difficult place for plants to grow.

Yet, rising out of the desert sand and scrub brush is an amazing sight—the giant saguaro (pronounced suh WAH row) cactus.

A saguaro can live as long as 200 years. It can grow to 50 feet tall (15 meters) and weigh as much as 10 tons (9 metric tons). That's the weight of three or four automobiles.

The elf owl is only 5 inches long (13 centimeters). It is the smallest owl in the world. The elf owl is only one of the many birds that find a safe, dry home inside the cool saguaro.

From all over the desert, animals and birds walk, crawl, and fly to the saguaro. That's because a saguaro is much more than just a giant plant. It is the center of life for hundreds of creatures, including this tiny elf owl.

Life for a new saguaro begins in the summer, when warm rains come to the desert. This is also when the bright, red fruit of a full-grown cactus falls to the ground. For desert creatures, it is time to feast!

Insects and birds feed on the sweet, juicy pulp of the saguaro's fruit. Mice and rabbits gobble up the soft, black seeds. By chance, a seed may stick to a mouse's paw or to a rabbit's ear. Perhaps the seed will travel with the animal to another place in the desert. And maybe it will fall to the ground and take root.

The desert is a harsh place for young saguaros. Most cactus seedlings die in the blazing heat. But a few lucky plants take root in shady spots, safe from the burning sun. In the shadow of a mesquite (mess KEET) tree, this ten-year-old saguaro is off to a good start.

The saguaro has long folds on its skin called pleats. These pleats allow the cactus to stretch. As it takes in water, the saguaro grows fatter and fatter. A fully grown saguaro can stretch until it holds several thousand pounds of water!

. . . .

The saguaro's roots do not grow deep. They stay shallow to catch any bit of rainwater that drips through the ground. The roots spread out as much as 90 feet (27.5 meters), forming the shape of a giant bowl.

The saguaro grows very slowly. After 50 years it stands only 10 feet tall (3 meters). Every spring lovely flowers appear. Each flower blooms for only one full day

On this day, birds, bats, and insects may come to drink the nectar. This is the sweet liquid inside a flower. As the creatures drink, bits of flower dust, called pollen, stick to their bodies. At the next flower, a bit of pollen might fall off and start a new cactus.

When there is no more nectar to drink, most of the creatures leave. But not the gila woodpecker. With its long, sharp beak the bird tap ... tap ... taps through the saguaro's tough skin to build a nest.

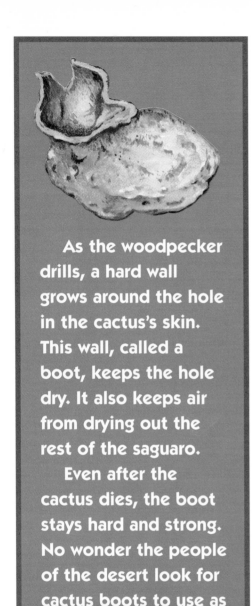

As the woodpecker drills, a hard wall grows around the hole in the cactus's skin. This wall, called a boot, keeps the hole dry. It also keeps air from drying out the rest of the saguaro.

Even after the cactus dies, the boot stays hard and strong. No wonder the people of the desert look for cactus boots to use as dishes and bowls!

Soon, the woodpecker has drilled a hole that reaches deep inside the cactus. The dark hole makes a cool nesting place for the woodpecker's family. Safely inside, the birds hunt and feast on insects that would otherwise harm the saguaro.

A woodpecker family does not stay in the same nest for long. When the babies are ready to fly, the family moves on. Soon the family is tapping a new hole either in that cactus or in another.

Old woodpecker nests do not stay empty. As soon as
one kind of bird moves out, another moves in. Elf owls are
among the first to take over. Unlike woodpeckers, however,
these little owls may stay in the same hole for years.

Other birds, such as this starling, follow close behind. High up in the spiny saguaro, the birds find a safe, cool place to raise their families.

At 60 years of age, the cactus is almost 18 feet tall (5.5 meters). Now branches reach out from its sides like arms. There, white-winged doves build cozy nests. Red-tailed hawks and horned owls also find homes on the growing saguaro. Somehow, the sharp spines of the cactus do not get in their way.

By the time it is 75 years old, the saguaro is nearly 50 feet tall (15 meters) . . . and teeming with life! It is more like a crowded village than a plant.

Birds aren't the only creatures in search of a cool cactus home. Lizards, insects, and spiders also fill empty nest holes. The insects feed on the cactus. The lizards and spiders feed on the insects.

Mule deer and other animals come to eat the tender plants that grow in the shade of the saguaro. Still other creatures, such as the ringtail cat, perch at the top. Up here, they stay safe from coyotes and are free to spy on small prey.

Keen-eyed coyotes and bobcats hunt in the brush around the saguaro. Perhaps one of them will dine on a jackrabbit tonight.

Coyotes are members of the dog family. Although they are excellent hunters, coyotes eat just about anything. Rabbits, gophers, rats, squirrels, reptiles, and insects are all food for coyotes. So are antelope, goats, and sheep. But when necessary, coyotes will even eat berries, melons, and beans!

For 150 years or more, the saguaro provides an important habitat for many desert creatures. But, in the end, old age and disease weaken the trunk of the great plant.

When this happens, desert winds topple the dead plant to the ground. Creatures living in the saguaro must move to a new cactus home.

Beneath the cactus's tough, spiny skin are long wooden ribs. These ribs hold up the giant plant. For hundreds of years they have been used by desert people for fences, roofs, and firewood.

After the saguaro dies, it is still necessary to desert life. Now the plant becomes a cool, shady home for creatures that live close to the desert floor.

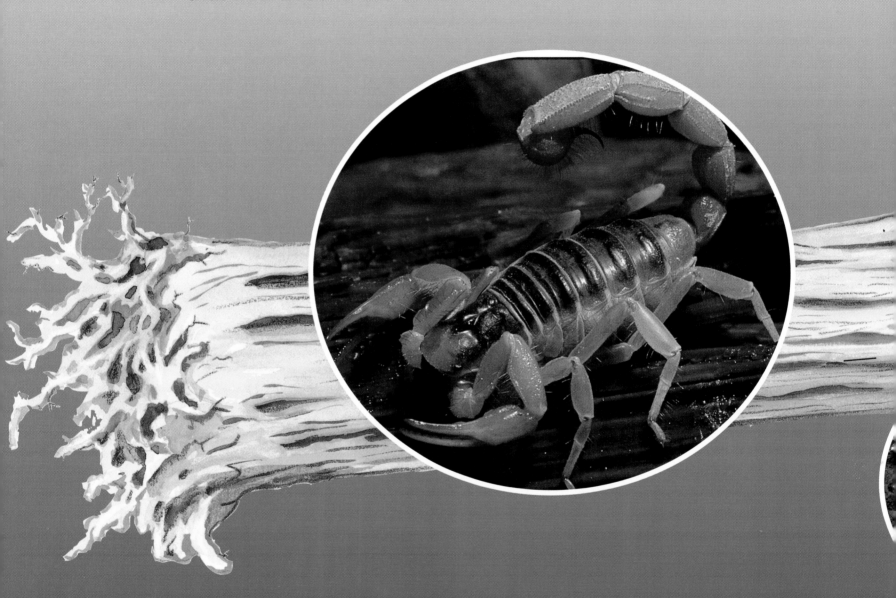

Among others, scorpions, rattlesnakes, and horned lizards come to the dead saguaro looking for food and shelter.

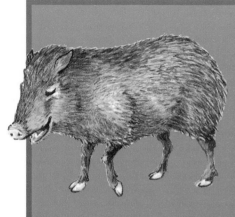

Javelinas are distant cousins of wild hogs. They have rough grayish black coats with silvery collars. Although javelinas feed mostly on roots, they sometimes prey on small animals.

Very, very slowly, the dead cactus decomposes, or rots away. Over time, it will return to the earth. For now, though, animals such as this javelina drop by. Using all its strength, the javelina tears at the fallen cactus. Could a meal of tender young plants lie beneath it?

But look! Just behind the javelina, a young, healthy saguaro is growing. Perhaps the javelina won't harm it.

With a good deal of luck, the young saguaro will continue to grow, upward and outward into a grand cactus. And if it succeeds, it too, will one day become home to the many creatures of the Sonoran Desert.

More About

Saguaro Forest (page 4)
Many saguaros grow in this part of the desert. None of the plants that grow here have leaves. If they did they would lose too much water and dry up.

Gila Woodpecker (page 12)
Both gila woodpecker parents share the task of feeding and caring for their young. But at night, the father may sleep in a separate hole near the nest.

Desert Tortoise (page 6)
With its strong legs and sharp claws, the desert tortoise is a great digger. At the end of fall, it digs a deep burrow in the sand where it will spend the winter.

Starling (page 17)
The starling originally came from Europe. In 1890, about 60 starlings were set free in Central Park in New York City. Millions of starlings now live in the United States.

Mesquite Tree (page 10)
The hardy mesquite tree grows where very few other plants can survive. It has many uses. Gum from its sap is even used to make candy!

Praying Mantis (page 20)
The praying mantis is a greedy hunter. It feeds on other insects, including other praying mantises. If they are hungry enough, females may even eat their mates.

This Habitat

Wolf Spider (page 20)
Wolf spiders are active hunters. Many stalk insects. They pounce on their prey the same way tigers do.

Horned Lizard (page 27)
The spines of the harmless horned lizard protect it from hungry animals. Some horned lizards also defend themselves by squirting little jets of blood from their eyes.

Bobcat (page 23)
Bobcats sneak around dead saguaros, hunting for mice, pack rats, rabbits, and other small animals. Their fine senses of sight and hearing help them to catch their prey.

Rattlesnake (page 27)
Rattlesnakes shed their skins two to four times each year. At each shedding they get one new rattle. Many rattlesnakes live in the Sonoran Desert.

Giant Scorpion (page 26)
The scorpion's stinger is at the end of its curved tail. Although painful, the sting of most American scorpions does not usually cause death.

Saguaro Cactus (page 29)
The giant saguaro is the largest cactus in the United States. One cactus can hold about 1,000 bathtubs full of water!